LUSTY LEOPARD'S
FIERY GIRL

COMPANY 417 SHIFTERS SERIES

AMELIA WILSON

CONTENTS

CHAPTER ONE

Iris

The voice on the other end of the line is about the most irritating voice as any voice has ever been. Of course, I feel that way whenever I deal with people like this so I guess there are a bunch of people with the most irritating voice in the world. I listen and finally say, "I understand your position but we'll need payment right now."

"Didn't you hear anything I just said?" the man on the line said. "I told you it's not possible. It's just not possible."

I send a quick message to the IT department and say, "I just don't believe you."

"What?" he sounds offended. "What do you mean?"

"I mean I don't believe you when you say it's not possible. I think what's really happening is that you're prioritizing us in a lower position than you should." I send an email to him while he processes that. "I just emailed you your total balance. We need you to pay the past due amount, the current balance, and a two-month deposit as well."

"What? It's like I'm talking to a wall! I can't even get the past due amount and you're adding the rest."

"Like I said. I don't believe you. Thanks for your time."

I hang up and take a sip of my coffee. Tina looks at me from where she sits across the room. She's easily the best executive assistant in the world so why she doesn't actually go work for a C-level executive is beyond me. She's beyond good. She's damned incredible. I'm lucky to have her. She glances at her phone just as my phone rings. "Nineteen seconds," she says. "It's a record."

I pick it up and even though I know exactly who it is, I answer with, "This is Iris Fletcher. How may I help you?"

"The software's down!" The irritating voice is now panicked.

"Wow," I say drily. "That must be frustrating!"

"The service agreement guarantees us no downtime!" he shouts. "This costs us almost eleven thousand dollars per hour!"

"Hmmmm," I reply. "Even during non-business hours?"

"Yes, for fuck's sake! There are no business hours with us!"

"Language, language! Wow. So, you'll lose two

hundred seventy-five thousand dollars in revenue in only twenty-four hours?"

"Yes, Jesus Christ! Why am I talking to you? Send me to whoever handles outages. Who do I need to talk to?"

"You're talking to her," I say, "and I need to tell you, I have to wonder why you didn't just pay the forty-nine thousand dollars past due balance when I first asked for it two weeks ago when I told you I was the new director of operations. Hell, now you're stuck paying almost two hundred thousand dollars with your current balance and the deposits."

"But I'm not paying for software that crashes! You're... supposed... Oh my God. You shut us off."

"Now if only you'd been that smart when I told you to pay your bill," I say. "If I were you, I'd get to your bank and make the wire. I think the cut-off is one o'clock to send the money, I mean the bank cutoff. We'll get a notice at about three. If we get the money, I'll put in the work order to get you back up and running."

"Jesus! You can't do this!"

"Actually, the same service contract that guarantees you no service outages also indicates we can pull the plug the second you're past due. I not only can do this but I am doing it. Lucky for you, I'm feeling merciful. We won't take the fourteen days the contract allows to get things up and running for you again. I'd get to the bank. Oh, and my tech department leaves at noon but I'm sure they'll get right to it tomorrow morning when they get in!"

"Why in the hell are you doing this?"

"I have a better question. Why didn't you try to take advantage of the last person in my position? What's the difference between me and the last director of operations? Is it my accent? Wait. I don't have one. Is it my tits? Is it the lack of a penis between my legs? No, it's not that because your top shareholder is a woman and she wouldn't put up with that. Maybe it's just the way you're spending so much money with the marketing firm because of the cute salesgirl you're screwing. Who knows? Well, whatever it is, I'll look forward to the wire and we'll do our best to get you up as quickly as we can."

I hang up and Tina says, "My God, I love you."

I smile and shake my head. "I did some experimentation in college but, nah, it's just not for me."

She groans at the joke and says, "Okay. Nine-Flux, Inc. They're the last significant aging. They owe twenty-eight thousand. That's two months. Name is Jack Harrison."

"Jack Harrison," I repeat. "Sounds like a movie star."

"Maybe you should ask him for a picture," Tina suggests.

"I might do that," I say.

I dial the number and a moment later, a tired-sounding middle-aged voice answers, "Nine-Flux, this is Jack."

"Mr. Harrison? This is Iris Montgomery with Seam-Tech. How are you today?"

He chuckles. "Well, I've had better days but I've had worse ones too."

"I can relate," I respond. "Well, Mr. Jackson, I hate to have to make a bad day worse, but unfortunately, I need to talk about the past-due balance on your account."

"Yes," he says. "I understand."

He sounds forlorn and I feel a pang of sympathy as I inform him the past-due balance is two months delinquent and we will need payment right away.

"Ahh," he says. "Right away?"

"I'm afraid so."

"All right," he says in a defeated tone. "I'll talk to the partners and see if we can move some money around. Can I call you back first thing tomorrow?"

The pang of sympathy becomes a wave of sympathy and I say, "Is everything okay, Mr. Harrison?"

"Well, not really," he admits. "There was some conflict among the shareholders which ended in a buyout of one of the major principals. It's all settled now but the buyout cost us millions. That's why we've been late."

"I see."

"I'm not trying to make excuses," Mr. Harrison says quickly. "We owe you that money and it's not your fault that one of the owners bailed on us. We'll figure something out."

"I'll tell you what," I say. "Don't worry about the twenty-eight thousand right now. Get me four thousand and you can spread the other twenty-four over your next twelve payments."

"Really?" Harrison asks. "Are you sure?"

"I'm sure," I say. "You're a good client and we want to

help in any way we can. If you get me four thousand by Monday and two thousand a month on top of your normal bill for the next twelve months, we're square."

"Thank you!" he says. "Yes, that'll—I think we can manage that, thank you!"

"You're welcome, Mr. Harrison. You take care now."

I hang up and smile. I glance at the door and see our intern, Derek, standing there, looking at me like I'm some kind of goddess.

Tina casts a similarly worshipful look at me and I feel a blush start to creep over me. "If you're waiting for me to sprout wings and a halo, you can save your breath."

"I think you're angel enough, already," Derek says.

He turns an adorable tomato-red color and I stifle laughter as I smile and say, "Thank you, Derek."

He nods quickly, then turns to leave. He stops, remembering something, and turns to me, staring at the floor and still blushing. "Umm, Mr. Hyde wants me to ask you if you can lead the finance discussion at the board meeting today."

I inwardly roll my eyes. There's nothing I love more than answering stupid questions from pompous old men who insist that a woman couldn't possibly know what she's talking about and must be mistaken on every point.

I keep my irritation hidden and smile sweetly at Derek. "Of course, Derek. Thank you."

He nods then literally runs out of the room. Tina and I burst out laughing and Tina says, "You're so mean! Why do you tease him like that?"

"Oh, it's harmless," I say. "He's a good kid, he deserves the ego boost."

"I'll bet that's not the only thing that's boosted."

"Now who's being inappropriate?" I print an agenda, then stand. "I'm going to make some copies for the meeting," I say. "If anyone calls back, tell them I'm screwing the intern and take a message."

Tina rolls her eyes. "You're horrible."

"And you love me." I walk into the copy room and start copying the agenda. I think about Jack Harrison and smile again. It felt nice to help someone out.

The fire alarm shrieks suddenly and I jump. My first thought is that someone pulled the alarm as a prank. I've heard of people in other offices doing things like that.

God! There is roaring in the air. That's the only way to describe how things sound. I rush to the door and push.

Nothing.

I'm confused and turn the handle. The door is unlocked. It won't move, though.

Then I smell the smoke.

CHAPTER TWO

Jeff

Nothing about this building makes sense. The third floor looks like a war zone but the first and second are nothing at all. The fourth floor is only scorched right now, although it will sustain more damage as the fire burns. All of the places where a fire might start accidentally are in the basement or on the first floor. Sure, there could be a trash fire in an office, or someone smoking indoors when they're not supposed to, but that wouldn't lead to explosive results. The same goes for electrical fires. This tells anyone with even a modicum of knowledge about fires and structures that what we're dealing with here is an intentionally set fire, arson.

I'm not an arson investigator. I'm just a firefighter. You fight enough fires, though, you don't need to be an arson investigator to figure this out. I look at the building.

It's likely going to be out of commission for weeks. Hell, the owners might have to raze it and build it again despite the damage being concentrated so high.

"Excuse me?" I turn and see a woman who looks shaken but safe. "Iris is still in there."

She looks at me and shaken turns into terrified. "Oh, God! Can she even still be alive?"

"Who's Iris?"

"My boss!" she says. "She was in the copy room. It got blocked off. I couldn't move things. I don't know what... God!"

I wave to a paramedic, who rushes over. I hand off the woman and head to the building. I know if my boss sees me, he'll tell me it's too dangerous. I wait until I'm through the door and on the third-floor landing in the stairwell before I say into my microphone, "Rescue on the third floor."

"What? I thought I had all of you out?"

"I'm on the third floor," I say.

"Damn it, can you get out?"

"There's a civilian trapped in here."

I'm intentionally giving as little information as possible as I navigate through the burning wreckage trying to determine what would be an appropriate place for a copy room. I ignore rooms with glass windows although most of them have already shattered. I finally come across a door with three file cabinets piled against it.

There's no way those file cabinets got there from any kind of blast from the fire.

My radio is burning up but I ignore it so that I won't have to be insubordinate. I reach down and push one of the file boxes. It's heavy as hell but I get it a few feet away. The next one has wheels, and once I have it righted, I push it away more easily. The third one is on fire and heavy. I hook the side of it with my axe and pull at an angle, and I make a little bit of headway but not enough. I can use the headway, though, and I wedge my axe into the space and use it like a crowbar to pry the thing away. There's only a foot and a half of clearance when I try the door.

It doesn't budge. I step back and slam my axe against the handle. It comes off and this time the door opens. Smoke lays thick over the room and see more pouring in from under the door on the opposite side.

I see Iris lying unconscious in the middle of the floor. I approach quickly and fit a respirator over her mouth and nose, relieved when I see the respirator fog up and know she's still breathing.

She's beautiful and I have to intentionally stand and head for the exit to avoid being distracted. It's hard to tell under these circumstances but she looks to be in her late twenties or early thirties. She has soft skin and delicate features, even covered with soot. Well, I guess I'm assuming her skin would be soft if I touched it. She has soft-looking skin, I suppose. Of course, this is what happens to my mind when I get hyper-focused in the middle of a fire. It's like my brain needs an unimportant focus to function effectively on the very important issue of getting us out of the building. As I reach the door, I hear a crash and a moment later, a wave of heat washes over my back. I don't have to look behind me to know the fire has burned the opposite door down and is now consuming the room.

I rush downstairs as more wood crashes down around me. The exit is covered in flame and I adjust Iris so I'm holding her against my chest, keeping her legs and head close to avoid burning her. I run through the doorway just before the cross-beam falls to the ground and keep running until I reach the engine.

"Jesus, Jeff!" Captain Hinckney says. "What the hell were you doing in there?"

Instead of responding, I lower Iris to the ground and call for a paramedic. Hinckney's eyes widen and he mutters, "Jesus Christ, where'd you find her?"

"Copy room," I say. "Got her out just before the room collapsed."

He shakes his head. "I ought to rip you a new one, but I'm guessing it won't do any good."

"No sir," I say.

"Although I could you know. You think you're badass but I'll go ursine over feline any day." He gives me a smile. The last comment is designed to let me know he's proud of me even though he can't say it officially. It's also a typical, good-natured jibe about the superiority of bear shifters compared to leopard shifters. You can probably guess which he is and which I am.

I hear the hum of the engine and a moment later a jet

of water pours into the building. The fire sizzles and snaps for a few moments but quickly quiets.

"What do you think?" Hinckney asks. "Arson?"

"I think so."

"Dammit," he says. "Just what we need."

"This is directed, though," I say, "not like that craziness from before. I mean, only one floor."

The paramedic arrives and begins examining Iris. After a few moments, she says, "This one got lucky. She's covered in soot and she'll need treatment for mild smoke inhalation, just in case, but she sustained only a few minor burns and no trauma. You got her out of there in the nick of time, Jeff."

"Glad to hear it."

I help the paramedic load her onto the stretcher. As I set her onto the gurney, her eyes flutter open and she stares at me.

For the first time in my life, I am speechless. Her eyes are like pools of light, soft and bright and beautiful and I am instantly lost.

"What happened?" she asks.

"There was a fire," I say. "You were trapped inside and I rescued you."

"My hero," she says before lapsing back into unconsciousness.

I watch as the paramedics wheel her away, still lost in those perfect eyes.

CHAPTER THREE

Iris

I stare up at the ceiling of the hospital room and reflect on being alive.

The ceiling, like the rest of the room and the rest of the building—at least the part visible through the small window at the top of the door, is painted the mellow off-white of nearly every hospital that doesn't cater specifically to children. Like the thin cotton gown I wear and the plastic mattress on which I lie, it serves as a visual reminder of just how close I came to death.

There are other, more sobering reminders, of course. The IV is out of my vein now but the stand with its half-full bag of fluid remains next to my bedside and I still wear the sensor on my finger for my oxygen level, along with several attached to my chest to monitor my breathing and my heart, but it's the beige paint and plastic bed that most starkly indicates to me that I'm lucky to be alive.

Lucky because of the firefighter.

I don't remember much about the man who rescued me. I remember the feel of his strong arms as they carried me out of the building. I remember the sound of his voice as he tells me he rescued me. I remember his piercing, steel-gray eyes and strong jaw. I remember thinking if angels exist, he must be one of them.

And then I'm in darkness.

Wonderful darkness.

I don't remember anything else until I woke up in the hospital the next day, covered in bandages and wearing a respirator and another IV in my arm. Tina is the first person to visit me and I feel bad because instead of being happy to see her, I'm disappointed that my rescuer wasn't there to welcome me back to the world of the living.

Tina tells me about the fire. The third floor is completely gutted and the fourth is badly burned as well. Tina says they nearly condemned the building due to concerns about structural damage but decided in the end that it was salvageable, though it will be several months before we can work there again.

I ask about my job and Tina very firmly tells me I will be doing nothing but, in her words, "Sitting on your ass and watching soap operas until the doctor tells me I can come back."

I smile and ask, "Do I look like the kind of girl who watches soap operas?"

She responds with, "Crime shows then. Or war movies. Or cartoons for all I care. The point is, you are not to touch a cell phone unless it's your doctor on the other end. *Capisce?*"

I smile and promise to be good.

I have no idea how I'm going to manage that. I'm already going stir crazy and I remain stir crazy as an entire godforsaken week passes before I get the beautiful news that makes me smile. The doctors are releasing me today and I'll get to go home. That's a plus but the thought of sitting at home all day doing nothing isn't much more appealing than lying in a hospital bed doing nothing.

The door opens and Tina walks in, followed by the discharge nurse. She grins when she sees me and wraps me in an embrace that only just manages to be gentle.

"Iris, you look so much better!" she cries.

"Really? I think I look like shit."

She scoffs. "You could swim through a sewer and you still wouldn't look like shit. How are you feeling?"

I shrug. "I'm all right. I mean, physically, I feel fine. I'm just not looking forward to convalescing."

"Tough," she says, putting her hands on her hips and staring sternly down at me. "Convalescing is all you're going to do until you're fully recovered. Got it?"

"Got it," I say. "But I don't have to be happy about it."

"I suppose not," Tina says.

"Hey, wait a minute," I say, "I just remembered something."

"What's that?"

"You work for me and not the other way around."

"You're still convalescing. You don't like it, you fire me."

"Yeah, yeah, yeah."

"Jesus, what a horrible time for this."

"Don't worry about it. All of the clients you were working on before the fire have paid the agreed-upon amounts and everyone who needed to be reinstated is up and running. We've already got the administration organized at the warehouse, and apart from operations not enjoying that all of the muckety mucks see them now, everything is fine."

"You only told me all that so I would be even more miserable not working."

She helps the discharge nurse load me into a wheelchair and a half hour later, she pulls into my driveway and helps me into the house. As soon as we're inside, I stand and walk to the kitchen for a glass of water, more to show Tina that I'm not an invalid than because I'm actually thirsty.

It takes another twenty minutes to convince Tina that she doesn't need to stay with me tonight but she finally leaves when I agree to let her check on me in the morning. I change out of the gown into sweatpants and a comfortable t-shirt, order takeout and turn the tv on but I can't focus on the crime show that's playing, even though it's one of my favorites.

My mind is filled with images of my rescuer. His strong jaw, piercing eyes, rock-hard body, and a voice that is soothing and commanding at the same time. I close my eyes and allow my hand to slip underneath my pants.

I move slowly, still weak from the smoke, but the image of my rescuer is enough to make up for any lack of strength on my part and my body responds almost immediately, sending warm tingling sensations through me from my toes to the crown of my head.

My nipples become instantly erect and I use the hand not stroking my clit to pinch one of them. I imagine my rescuer's lips sucking on my nipple while his hand massages my pussy and gasp as electric shocks pulse between my clit and my nipple.

"Oh..." I start to moan, then realize I don't know his name. "Oh, baby," I finish. That's good enough for a fantasy.

My hand moves faster and I feel my pussy start to tighten, so I lower my other hand from my breast and slip a finger inside my pussy. Having something to squeeze causes my pussy to tighten considerably and when I slip a second finger inside and start slowly massaging my g-spot in time with my clit, my pussy shivers and pulses and my stomach tightens until finally, I scream as my climax shoots through me like a rocket and I collapse onto my back, still rubbing until the sensation is finally too intense and I have to pull my fingers away from my clit.

It's several more minutes before my pussy relaxes enough that I can remove my fingers and when they brush against my clit I gasp as an aftershock runs through me.

My phone rings then. I look at the number. I don't

recognize it and I'm about to follow Tina's advice and let it go to voicemail but something inspires me to answer. I do and gasp when I hear a voice that shouldn't be so familiar but is nonetheless burned into my mind.

"Hello?" my rescuer asks. "Is this Iris Fletcher?"

"It—this is she," I say breathily.

"I'm Jeff O'Leary," he says. "I'm the firefighter who rescued you last week."

"I know who you are," I say.

"Oh, good," he says. He pauses a moment, then adds, "Listen, I don't want to bother you but I was wondering if I could stop by later to talk? I wanted to see how you were doing and maybe talk a little bit about what happened and see if there's anything I can do to help."

I can think of some ways for him to help.

"Of course," I respond. I make my voice a little sultry and add, "You know, you never gave me the chance to thank you properly."

He pauses again, then replies. "Well, we can talk about that too."

Another aftershock runs through my pussy and I bite my lip to keep from moaning into the phone. "Well, then. When should I expect you, Jeff O'Leary?"

"I'll be there tomorrow late afternoon. Will that work?"

"That sounds perfect," I respond. I give him my address and say, "I'll see you soon."

"Okay," he says. "I'll see you then."

He hangs up and I'm so turned on by the exchange that my hand once more lowers to my pussy.

Of course, that's when the doorbell rings. My takeout has arrived.

I sigh and dress myself. "Coming!"

CHAPTER FOUR

Jeff

I lower my nose to the ground and quickly pick up the scent of bighorn sheep. There are four individuals present but the one I'm interested in is a mature ram, at least two hundred fifty pounds, and either in a rut or nearly so. He will be a formidable opponent.

Not too formidable, however. In animal form, I have the build and proportions of a typical leopard but while an average male leopard will weigh somewhere around one hundred twenty pounds, I tip the scales at closer to five hundred.

Shifters are always larger in animal form than the animals they shift into. No one's sure exactly why that is but it's true for every shifter regardless of the animal form they take. One of the men in my company is a black bear shifter who is so large that when he was seen by a pair of hikers in these mountains, he fueled rumors that large grizzlies had returned to the area for the first time in nearly two hundred years.

The ensuing rush of wildlife trackers and tourists essentially closed the area to shifters for the next several months and got my friend into a lot of trouble with the other local shifters. That wasn't quite as bad as one of my best friend's grandfathers. He's a puma shifter, a mountain lion. He was up in Alberta and got caught on camera. That was back in the eighties and naturalists thought there had to be a surviving Smilodon population. That's saber-tooth tigers. The truth is, there is a surviving population, but only the shifter version. I work with one. That place was lost to shifters, though, and he was persona non grata in Canada for a while.

That's another thing about shifters. We're very private and for good reason. Interactions between humans and shifters rarely end well for shifters. Either humans react in fear and try to kill us or drive us away or they treat us like gods and expect us to perform miracles ranging from the irritating to the outlandish. So, we've learned its best if we keep that side of our lives to ourselves and when we do shift, it's far from anyone who might see an unusually large animal and start putting two and two together. Of course, the cat's out of the bag now, no pun intended. We're officially out in the open as far as legal status and such but that doesn't change perceptions and most of us still hide what we are. Wouldn't you?

I bound up the mountain swiftly but quietly, my

padded feet allowing me to move my bulky frame around without making noise. I feel the same rush of adrenaline I always feel when I'm in this form. It's a sense of release and freedom—like I'm release from the chains of my human form and able to move and run the way I'm supposed to. Some shifters believe that we are animals at our core and it is our human forms and not our animal forms that are the deviation. I don't entirely agree with that but there's no mistaking that physically, at least, I'm happier as a leopard.

The scent of the sheep grows stronger and I can sense my prey is near. I slow to a crawl so I can be as silent as possible and stalk slowly over a large rock.

The sheep are on the other side—two ewes and a kid hiding behind a ram who stands in front of them, head lowered, braying loudly. It's a stance of challenging but not at me. In front of him, another cat stands, shoulders bunched and head lowered, ready to pounce.

This cat is not a shifter but a regular cat, a mountain lion. A big male, maybe as much as one hundred fifty pounds, and solidly built for the typically sleek species. He hasn't noticed me, his attention focused completely on the kill.

I growl softly and all five animals jerk towards the noise. The lion snarls at me, irritated at having his hunt interrupted. I stand tall and step forward so my larger size is clearly evident and growl again, more loudly this time.

The cat sizes me up and realizes he has no chance. He snarls irritably and bounds off, leaving me alone with the sheep. I drop from the rock and prepare to strike. The ram stares at me, his confidence gone. While he would have stood a slight chance against a mountain lion, he has no such chance against me. He lowers his head and snorts, driven by instinct to fight even though he knows he will certainly die.

Something unusual happens then. An image comes to my mind of Iris lying helpless on the floor of the copy room. I think about her lying helpless and vulnerable and my desire to hunt disappears. I turn from the ram and leap back to the top of the rock, then run into the forest.

This never happens. When I'm in shifter form, I still have my human cognition and intellect but my instincts and emotion are ruled by the animal form. I don't take joy in killing, per se, but I certainly don't feel any mercy for the prey I take.

I run back to the clearing where I've parked my SUV and shift back into human form. With my mind clear of animal instinct, I realize that what I feel isn't mercy but concern. I realize as well that thinking about Iris isn't surprising at all, leopard form or not. I haven't stopped thinking about her since the fire. Her soft skin and beautiful eyes, her angelic voice, and the way she smiled at me when she called me her hero. I want to see those eyes and that smile, feel that skin on mine.

I push that thought away and instead focus on the other reason I want to see her. So far, the arson investigation has yielded nothing helpful other than that propane was used as the accelerant. That means that anyone with a gas barbecue could have started the fire. In other words, we have nothing. The arson squad is treating it like a typical pyromania thing—some kid loves fire, likes burning things, wants to see if he can burn something bigger than a match—no motive other than liking the sight of flame a little too much.

I don't buy that. No random pyromaniac is going to waste time stacking furniture in front of a room before torching a place. Someone knew Iris was in there and deliberately trapped her there so the fire would kill her.

I call the number Iris's assistant, Tina, gave me, pulling it from where I put it in my wallet on the day of the fire. Iris answers quickly and the sound of her voice is enough to pull the other reason for seeing her to the front of my mind. We talk briefly and she says we're still on for me to drop by in a few hours. When I put my phone down, I groan and roll my eyes. Having just shifted, I spoke to her completely naked. Her voice had an obvious effect. I almost feel embarrassed as I have to tuck myself in to get my boxer shorts and jeans up on me.

I drive to my place first to shower and change, all the while struggling to keep my mind on the case and t Iris's body. I don't succeed at that, so I settle for thinking about both things at the same time and choosing to focus on the case.

I reach the address she gives me exactly three hours after the phone call. It's a nice ranch house with plenty of large windows, a long roof that provides generous shade, and a modestly sized but well-appointed front yard with a well-kept lawn and several planters containing yucca, cactus, and agave.

I walk to her door and knock. She opens and before I can speak, her arms are around me and her lips are on mine.

When she pulls away, she looks into my eyes with her own sunlit ones and says, "You saved me."

Then she kisses me again and pulls me inside.

CHAPTER FIVE

Iris

This is happening.

Oh my God, this is actually happening.

I pull away from Jeff's lips long enough to lift his shirt over his head and pause longer to allow my hands to explore his chiseled abs and powerful chest. When I fantasized about him earlier, I imagined him with the sculpted body of a Greek god. That fantasy doesn't do him justice. Maybe the king of the Greek gods. Maybe whatever the Greek gods worship as a god.

"What are you?" I breathe in wonder.

A look passes over his face then. It's a dangerous look, a predatory look, but I don't feel unsafe. Instead, I am more turned on than I've ever been and when he growls and tears my shirt away, I gasp and moan. He looks at me the way a lion looks at his prey and I resist the urge to throw myself at him, instead slipping fingers under the waistband of my panties and slowly pulling them down as I back toward the sofa.

He watches as I slowly reveal my body and when I finally let my skirt drop down to my ankles, he rushes me again and any semblance of control I thought I might have disappears as he crushes me to him and kisses me deeply and powerfully. This kiss is a kiss that... Well, damn, there's no real way to describe it. It's like staking a claim or planting a flag at the summit of a mountain. This kiss declares possession, and for now, at least for this moment, it's entirely appropriate because I belong to him completely.

His hands travel over me hungrily, exploring every part of me and I feel almost as though I'm near-climax, even though he hasn't directly stimulated anything sexual. I moan and pull away from his lips, whispering in his ear, "I need you inside me."

He growls into my ear, "Later."

Then he lifts me up into the air. I cry out in surprise and the cry is stifled when he pulls forward me forward and then lifts me up. My legs end up resting over his shoulders as he closes his mouth around me. My hands move to his head but not out of desire but just because suddenly I'm suspended in the air and I need the balance.

"Oh my God," I breathe. Then I can't say anything else but can only gasp and twitch as his lips and tongue delicately explore my folds, sliding over my lips and gently flicking my clit. The teasing, gentle way he does this is so vastly different from everything else but on the same token, it fits with the whole idea that at the moment, I belong to him. After all, if I belong to him, he can do whatever the hell he wants with me, and that includes this insane, desperation-inducing teasing.

God, it's almost unbearable! I need so much more but I also can't imagine anything better than exactly what happens at the moment. Sparks seem to run through me in a thousand different directions, causing me to shudder and writhe over him. He holds me upright with seemingly no effort and the knowledge he's holding me in the air while he goes down on me intensifies the experience.

"Oh, Jeff," I moan. He keeps it up and I continue to moan and occasionally whisper or even shriek his name. It's almost incomprehensible and I don't know how long it goes on. It sure as hell feels like I'm right on the edge of orgasm for an eternity.

And then, he pulls his mouth from my pussy, growls, "Cum for me, Iris," and then immediately drops back to my folds.

At his command, pins and needles begin to travel from the soles of my feet up my legs. At the same time, a warm sensation forms in my lower belly just above my pussy. My toes curl and my back arches as the sensations intensify for several excruciating seconds before finally releasing in an avalanche of pleasure.

I cry out, gasping and moaning, as my body shudders over him. My legs pound on his back as they shiver and my back arches and folds as my stomach clench with the force of each shock of the climax. My fingers tighten in his hair dramatically and it's a wonder I don't just end up yanking out big clumps.

He keeps licking and suckling softly, teasing my clit and keeping me at peak for far longer than normal. The sensation is almost unbearably pleasant and I push weakly at his face, trying to escape that godlike, incredible, perfect mouth and—

"God!" I cry as my orgasm peaks again.

That cry is also stifled as, without warning, he drops me from his shoulders and straight onto his cock. My eyes and mouth fly open and I stare wordlessly at him as he thrusts deep and hard into me.

Entering me in the midst of orgasm as he does extends my climax and my legs continue to spasm as my pussy and clit both shiver and pulse, struggling to cope with the sensations that run through me. He stares at me with his dark, predatory eyes and I shiver as I finally crest and come down from the peak, jerking and moaning and gripping his arms to try to gain some semblance of control over my body.

He groans and his movements become more urgent and though I'm still twitching, I squeeze my pussy as tightly as I can and repeat over and over, "Yes, yes, cum in me. Cum in me, baby."

I press my hand against his belly just above his shaft and begin to massage him in slow, deep circles. He cries out and shudders and drives himself deeply in me. I keep my eyes fixed on his face, watching his expression as he empties himself into me. I grind my hips and continue to massage his belly until I can no longer feel his cock pulsing inside me. Then, I cup my hand under his chin and kiss him while I grip his cock with my pussy and slowly pull off of him. I realize the strangeness of this entire thing happening while he stands. I've never had sex standing and hell, I wasn't even standing. Even now, my legs are wrapped around his body.

He kisses me and then slowly lowers me to the sofa.

I'm not finished with him yet, so as soon as I'm on the couch, I close my lips around him. He quickly hardens and I love the thought that for a moment at least, I'm in control. He allows it and I don't really know how long I work my lips and tongue on him. It could be an hour or only a few minutes later when he's pulsing inside my mouth as I swallow rhythmically and caress his balls.

After, he collapses to the couch next to me. "Wow."

"You can say that again," I say.

"Wow."

I roll my eyes. "So, rescuer. To what do I owe the pleasure of this visit? Other than this, I mean." I pat his cock.

He chuckles. "Actually, I wanted to talk to you about the fire."

My brow furrows. "The fire? Why?"

"Have they told you anything about the fire?"

"Tina told me it was arson if that's what you mean."

"Yes, but that's not all."

"What is it?"

He hesitates again, then says. "The door to the copy room was blocked when I got there."

"That's why I couldn't open it," I say, "Okay, but what does that have—" Then I realize. My eyes widen in horror and I finish with, "Oh, God."

He takes my hand and stares at me, once more wearing that predatory look. "Iris, listen. I promise you. No one is ever going to hurt you again."

He says it with such strength that even though I barely know him, I believe him completely. I relax and he smiles at me. The smile is gentle and kind and is such a contrast to the fierce look he wore earlier that I wonder if such opposite feelings can exist in the same man.

It fades a moment later, replaced with an almost apologetic look. "I hate to have to ask this, Iris, but can you think of anyone who might want to kill you?"

I laugh. "Ha! It might be easier to give you a list of people who don't want to kill me." He frowns and I quickly say, "Just joking. That was a joke."

"Not funny," he says but he's smiling. "Seriously, though. Think hard, here."

I think for a moment. "Umm, I don't know. There are a lot of people who might be angry with me."

"Like who?"

"Well, for starters, there's the old CEO, VP of Finance, and the guy who had my job before me. They were all fired and replaced with me, the new CEO, and the new VP."

"Did any of them say anything to you?"

I shake my head. "I mean, they talked to me but nobody seemed to blame me for it. Even the guy who had my job didn't act like it was my fault. I mean, in the meeting where it happened, everyone was there. They were pleasant enough under the circumstances. I think they knew it was coming for some time."

"And there's no one else who might want to hurt you?"

I shrug. "I mean, there's at least one delinquent account that probably wouldn't shed a tear if I died."

"What account is that?"

"Redwood Financial. I called to collect their past due balance earlier that morning and I was a little forceful. I really doubt they would go that far, though. To be honest, there are probably others, too. We came in to fix the company. It's that simple. One of the things that needed to be fixed was that they handled billing terribly and let people get away with not paying. A number of customers got rude awakenings in the weeks since I arrived. It cost all of them more than they owed, too." I sigh and say, "I wouldn't have imagined they would try to kill me."

"Okay, that's a start. Maybe someone wanted to hurt the business?"

"Dumb way to do it. Ninety-nine percent of the records are digital and all of the real work is done at the warehouse. It's not really a warehouse. That's just what we call it. The office that burned was just sales and administration. Someone who wanted to hurt the company would have hit the warehouse and... Well, that makes it clear." I sigh and say, "so they really were after someone in the office." I don't know why I can't just say the fire was about me.

He nods, then smiles again. "Well, no need to worry about that right now. The important thing is, you're alive and safe now."

"Yes," I say. I let my hand travel down his chest. "Thanks to you."

I spend a few minutes on my knees thanking him, then he carries me to bed and we spend far, far longer enjoying being alive before falling asleep in each other's arms.

CHAPTER SIX

Jeff

I bask in the afternoon sun atop a ledge some fifty miles or so from the city, close enough that I can still see the skyline from my vantage point but far enough away from both the city and the nearest road that it's very unlikely that anyone would spot a tiger-sized leopard lazing around on top of a rock.

I yawn and stretch, splaying my claws for maximum release. When I'm finished, I stand and lope off into the forest. I'm in a good mood. I've been in a good mood for the past four weeks.

Iris and I have seen each other nearly every day since that first visit, only missing two days when Company 417 was sent to a neighboring county to help fight a brush fire. Other than that, my free time has been mostly spent with her.

She's perfect.

Not only is she beautiful beyond words, but she's also the most intelligent and strongest person I've ever met. She takes the news that someone may have tried to kill her with far less fear than I expect. She is anxious to return to work and fumes at being cooped up in the house all day.

Her doctors want her to wait at least another two weeks to return to work and though I don't express this to Iris, I am glad she's remaining home a while longer even if she somehow got hooked up so she can work from her living room and isn't really obeying doctor's orders. The arson investigation is ongoing and my own investigation has yielded nothing so far.

I talk to Redwall Financial the day after I first visit Iris but I quickly realize they had nothing to do with the fire. Their controller waxes eloquent about his hatred of "that smug bitch" but when I inform him that Iris nearly died in the fire, he expresses genuine remorse and apologizes for calling her a bitch. I can detect no trace of deception in his voice or scent and further snoop around the building yields nothing suspicious.

His scent.

The truth is most shifters don't maintain any of their animal senses while in human form. Oh, certainly, some traits seem similar. All of the felines seem a bit cat-like. We all tend to be pretty physically fit although you wouldn't know that from the body shape of an elephant shifter. Still, the horse shifters look like runners. The bear shifters look like wrestlers. The cat shifters... Well, we tend to look like predators. Dragon shifters... Hell, they look regal, I guess. There are so many shifters and they all have characteristics of the animal but few have the senses or skills of the animal when in human form. Leopards are an exception. We tend to retain our sense of smell. It seems damned strange that we do but shifters with animals more renowned for that don't. In any case, I neither hear nor smell deception.

My other leads turn up empty as well and I am becoming frustrated. Iris returns to work in a few weeks and I'll have less control over her surroundings and be less able to protect her.

I growl, startling a ground squirrel back into its hole. I shift back into human form and walk the rest of the way to my car, breathing deeply to calm myself. I'm calm by the time I reach the truck but I'm also resolved to talk to the investigators. It's taking too long to figure this out. As I do, I find myself hoping that the lion from the other day might show up and see a naked human as easy prey. It's a silly, overly aggressive thing to want to kill a cat just so I can work out some frustration but, on the other hand, worry about that girl is getting to me.

The division headquarters where the arson office is located in a few miles closer to downtown than my station and with the afternoon traffic, it takes me over an hour to drive there. I call Iris on the way and chat with her for a few minutes. Hearing her voice calms me and I'm in a better mood when I reach the office.

I walk to the front desk and introduce myself then ask to speak to Arson.

The desk officer calls ahead and asks me to take a seat.

"I'll stand," I say.

She looks at me but doesn't say anything.

A moment later, her phone rings and she announces that Arson will see me.

The lead investigators are standing around the desk. Behind the desk, sits Captain Rosenthal, the chief of the investigation Division.

Mulgrew, the oldest of the leads, smiles at me. "Good afternoon, O'Leary. I heard about your heroic rescue at the SeamTech fire last week. Outstanding job."

"Thank you, sir," I say.

"It's moments like that that make me proud I joined the Department," chimed in Davis, another investigator.

"Thank you, but I'm not here to talk about myself," I say. "I want to see how the Arson investigation is progressing."

They exchange looks with each other. Then Holden, the youngest investigator and the closest to me in age says, "Jeff, don't worry man, we've got this. We'll figure out who did it and we'll get them off the streets."

"Does that mean you know what happened?" I demand.

"The investigation is ongoing," Holden said tolerantly, "But we'll find the perpetrator eventually."

"Eventually might be too late," I say, growing frustrated. "Iris... Miss Fletcher is still in danger."

They exchange knowing looks and Davis says, "Jeff, these kinds of things are usually kids or disturbed people who have a fire fixation. Pyros, you know. They don't target people. They just like to watch things burn. And they never hit the same place twice. He might light something again, but it won't be your girlfriend's workplace."

"So, you're not even considering the possibility that she could have been targeted directly?"

Mulgrew sighs. "No, Jeff, we're not considering it."

"Why not?"

"Because it's just not true," Davis says. "Look, Jeff—"

"The copy room was blocked, Captain," I say, ignoring Davis and speaking straight to Captain Rosenthal.

"It's a fire," Holden said. "Things burn and fall over and block doorways."

"That's not what happened here," I insist. "Nobody blocked that doorway by accident."

"Look, Jeff—"

I narrow my eyes and growl, "If I hear 'Look, Jeff,' one more time, I'm going to tear someone's throat out."

Captain Rosenthal speaks. "Wind down, O'Leary." His tone is unmistakable.

I clench my jaw and my fists a moment but then nod and will myself to relax. "I'm concerned that Miss Fletcher's safety isn't being taken seriously," I say.

"If you're concerned for Miss Fletcher's safety, you should consult the police," Rosenthal said. "And if you're concerned about the arson investigation, you should allow the arson investigators to do their jobs and stop insisting that they waste time on your assumptions."

"It's not an assump—"

"How many weeks did you spend training for your job?" he interrupts.

"Seventeen weeks at the academy, like everyone else."

"And you've got three exemplary years behind you, too," he says. "Every one of the members of my team did that same seventeen weeks but they did it after they went through the police academy and spent time in detective squads. If a fire broke out at my house and my family was there, I'd hope like hell your squad got the call and you showed up. This isn't your wheelhouse. It's ours."

I sigh and say, "I just have a hard time thinking this is regular arson." I shrug.

"Thank you, O'Leary." His voice softens a bit. "You're a good firefighter, Jeff, but this is our job. We're good at it. Don't worry. We'll figure out who did it."

I nod and force a smile before walking out. I am fuming and when I leave, I drive straight back to the forest, strip, shift, and go for a run.

As I bound through the trees, I think about Iris. Someone is trying to hurt her. Someone wants her dead.

My eyes narrow and I quicken my speed. That someone will wish they'd never been born when I find them.

CHAPTER SEVEN

Iris

I stand and take a long, satisfying stretch.

I'm back, baby.

Well, okay, I'm not actually back. The third-floor offices are still closed, and I had to work a compromise to work three days at home and two at the office every week. That isn't about my health. It's about the limited office space available at the warehouse. Part of my job is finding a good office lease for us. Still, it feels so much better to be doing something officially rather than getting yelled at every day for the work I do at home.

Can't say I have any complaints about the way I've been spending my nights, though.

Jeff is wonderful, beyond belief, incredible, whatever other superlative you can think of. He's sexy as hell, and I won't pretend that orgasms aren't part of what makes him so amazing.

That's not all of it, though. He's the perfect man. Like, literally the perfect balance of everything that makes a man wonderful. He's strong, sexy, and protective and when we make love, he has an almost animal-like aggressiveness that turns me on to no end. At the same time, he's gentle and kind and adorably concerned with my comfort and happiness.

He's a fantasy in bed and a dream out of bed.

God, I sound like a teenager with a diary.

I can't help it, though. I think I might be falling in love for the first time in my life. Jeff is everything I could have ever asked for in a man and more.

The best part is that I feel safe with him.

I don't know for sure that I agree with Jeff that someone's trying to kill me. It seems like a stretch, even considering how much of a hard ass I am sometimes. I could see someone trying to sue me but trapping me in a room and burning the building down around me? That's psycho lover territory and not disgruntled former employee territory.

Still, the thought that there might be someone out there who would think to do that to me is sobering and knowing I have Jeff there to protect me is the most reassuring thing I can think of. I can't point my finger at exactly why, other than his impressive physique. He's not a soldier or a police officer. He's a firefighter.

There's something about him, though, something

besides his physical prowess that makes me feel like no one can hurt me when I'm with him. Something in the look in his eyes when we together communicate to me that I am his and he will protect what is his.

It's quite possibly the sexiest part about him.

I pull myself away from my thoughts and dial Tina. She answers in a peppy voice, "Iris! I'm so glad you called!"

"So, you found them?"

"Nope!" she says brightly.

I roll my eyes. "You're hilarious, you know that?"

She giggles. "That's why you love me."

"I also love you because you're good at your job," I say.

"I can be amazing at my job and still not find something that isn't there," Tina says. "What exactly are we looking for again?"

"Accounting receipts, invoices, bills of sale, financial reports, anything that might explain where all the missing money went."

"And we're absolutely sure money's missing?" Tina asks dubiously.

"Either money's missing or someone's really bad at math," I say, "But there are nearly three million dollars of missing money from last year's balance sheet and I need to figure out where that went."

"If you say so, boss."

I smile. "If you find something, I'll take you out for ice cream, how's that?"

"You'll take me out for ice cream whether I find anything or not," she says, "Making me prowl around this storage unit all day. You know it's like the size of a small warehouse, right?"

"That's why I have my best employee on the job," I say.

"Yeah, yeah," she says.

"Give it today and tomorrow," I say, "and after that, if we still can't find it, we'll hire James Banks for a day to help us locate things." Banks is the man I replaced.

"You think he won't mind?"

"We're a pretty critical part of his resume. Besides, everyone knew what was coming. It'll probably be an ego boost for him. I know Brad called in Francis for a day and paid him \$2500 for consulting as he wrapped his head around things. He said if Leo and I needed to do the same, we could."

"Well, if it's good enough for the dynamo CEO, I guess it's good enough for the slave driver director of operations," Tina says.

"I love you, Tina!" I say sweetly.

"We'll test that theory when it's ice cream time," she says and then hangs up.

I start calling clients and following up on accounts that have gone delinquent in the past our weeks. There are always a few odd accounts that end up behind. Usually, the conversation goes as it did with Nine-Lux. We talk through it, and I help them find a repayment plan that works for them. Occasionally, the conversation goes more like Redwall and I have to be a little firmer.

In between calls, I gather what little data I still have on my investigation. I hate to throw around words like fraud and embezzlement but at this point, I'm not really sure what else to call it. I suspect that Jeff is at least partly right and someone burned the office to burn the financial records, although I'm still not convinced that I was targeted specifically.

I wonder what would lead someone to steal that much money. I understand the appeal of wealth, but that seems like such a risk to take for a nicer house and a fast car.

My phone buzzes. It's a text from Jeff. *Dinner tonight?*

I text back *sounds delicious!*

He responds with *You sound delicious.*

I smile and reply, *maybe after dinner, I'll let you have some dessert.*

He sends *I can't wait.*

I smile and think about Jeff's mouth on my pussy, licking and sucking and massaging expertly. I close my eyes and let my hand travel down in between my legs. I gasp when they reach their destination. I moan and settle back in my chair, allowing my fingers to travel freely over my clit. I let my other hand travel over my body, imagining Jeff's hands on me while his tongue stimulates my clit.

I imagine his lips closing around my pussy as he licks and sucks and soon, I cry out and clamp my thighs together as I cum. I jerk so hard that I fall out of the office chair and land heavily on the floor.

I start laughing at myself as I pick myself up, still shivering from the orgasm and of course, that's when my phone decides to ring. It's Tina.

"I found it!" she says brightly.

"Fantastic!" I say. "What do you have?"

"Umm, receipts mostly and accounting invoices."

"That's perfect! What's the date range?"

"Looks like February through October."

"That's good," I say. "That's a solid start. Can you bring it by tomorrow?"

"Tomorrow? Why not tonight."

I blush a little. "I have plans tonight."

She squeals and says, "With the fireman?"

"Yes, with Jeff! We've been dating for two months, you know that."

"I know, I just like living vicariously through you," she says. "Seriously, though, I'm happy for you. Have fun tonight. I'll see you tomorrow."

"Goodbye," I say.

I hang up and get ready for dinner, then wait anxiously until my doorbell rings. I quickly answer and Jeff stands there, wearing a perfectly tailored suit with his hair neatly groomed.

He smiles and says, "Are you ready for dinner?"

I reach forward and grab his necktie, pulling him inside the door. "I think I'll take dessert first," I say.

CHAPTER EIGHT

Jeff

I feel like I'm hitting a wall, and the thing that makes no sense to me at all is how in the world you can find a needle in a haystack when you don't even know if it's a needle and there are thousands of haystacks all around. I don't have any idea how to proceed, and I especially don't know how I'm supposed to protect Iris if I can't determine the threat.

While these thoughts fill my mind, my phone rings. The caller ID tells me it's the Fire Department's main office. I answer with, "Firefighter O'Leary."

"Jeff," the voice says. I don't recognize it right away. "This is Rosenthal."

"Captain," I say, "Hello. What can I do for you, sir?"

"I just wanted to tell you that you were right."

"Sir?"

"Well, nine-hundred and ninety-nine times out of a thousand, arson isn't about murder, at least not targeted, but you were right. We found letters from an intern. The guy was obsessed with that girl. We're talking love letters he wrote but never sent. The idiot had them in a lockbox on his desk, it was a cheap lockbox but the fire didn't burn too badly there and the letters survived."

"Jesus," I say. "You got him?"

"Yes. He's in custody. We interviewed a few people and they said he always seemed overly enthusiastic. The guy she replaced said he intended not to renew the intern's job. I guess it's set on a rolling three-month thing. Then he got fired, though, so the intern stayed. Anyway, I wanted to let you know. You're eligible for the arson squad next year. I hope you'll think about it."

"Captain, I don't know what to say. Thank you."

"Say you'll think about it."

"Yes sir."

I hang up and let out a whoop. Ricardo, who is busy with hose maintenance looks over at me from the other end of the truck bay. "God, shut up, you damned spotted dork. Some of us are trying to work."

"You're just jealous your spots get lost in your coat," I yell back.

Someone inside yells, "All you cats are the same!"

I glance at the clock. I've got a few hours before I can leave but I text Iris and tell her I have updates. She calls me immediately. "About Derek, right?" she asks.

"Yeah," I say. "So, you heard from the arson squad?"

"No. I heard from James Banks."

"A detective?"

"No. He had the job before me. We needed some help to track down some documents in the storage unit and when I called him, he told me how he was interviewed. I guess they found threatening letters?"

"I think they more obsessed than threatening but that's pretty much the same thing."

"No, I don't think it is. I know of a firefighter who's totally obsessed with me. I mean, apart from the chance of my heart stopping from the sheer audacity of his sense of humor, I'm not in any danger."

"So, it's really over?"

"Looks like it is, beautiful," I say, "I'm off in a couple of hours. What if I take you out for a nice dinner to celebrate?"

"What if we order bad takeout and stay in to celebrate?" she replies.

"God, I love you," I say.

She doesn't respond.

Dear God, did I just say what I think I just... Holy shit.

I open my mouth to backtrack as fast as humanly possible but then she says, "I love you, too, Jeff."

There's no real way to describe how that feels except maybe what it's like when I have an itch on my side and I rub up against a tree and it hits the right spot, how it takes an uncomfortable situation and puts everything right in the world. "Well then," I say, "I think staying home to celebrate is absolutely the right thing to do."

There's a moment of silence and she finally says, "Wow. Things... Just wow." I can hear the wonder in her voice. She sounds almost giddy.

I sail through the rest of the day and the celebration is about as perfect as any celebration can be. In fact, there are three weeks of celebrations, broken only by the times I'm stuck sleeping at the station. It's wonderful to start thinking in terms of forever with her instead of right now. I am definitely well past the idea of enjoying our time together and right in the can't live without her zone. As far as I'm concerned, she's amazing in every conceivable way. She's amazingly beautiful. She's amazingly engaging. She's amazing when she's serious and amazing when she's funny. As far as what she does for a living, I know it's something I could probably never accomplish with the skill and success she accomplishes it. That's one thing I find really remarkable.

It's amazing to talk with her about turnarounds, the kind of thing she does. She's had nine jobs in the last four years, each time coming in as part of a team to fix a company on the verge of ruin. It's truly remarkable, actually, how she does it. I can understand why she talks about having a lot of enemies but the truth is, she bruises egos but essentially saves companies. I find it all fascinating, especially when she explains the skill set that will get a company from nothing to a million dollars in sales a year is entirely different from what will get it to five million, which is different from what will get it to twenty-five million. Most people can't understand how the hard work they put in for years to get a company to one point can actually bring it right to the brink of bankruptcy in the next stage of growth. The last eight companies are thriving now. The ninth is on its way to thriving.

Really, from what I can see, she might hurt some feelings but it makes a great deal of sense that the guy who went after her is just a whack job. On balance, people end up very grateful to her and the team. They rescue legacies. It's probably too dramatic of me to say her people are like firemen for businesses but it's not too far from the truth. Of course, she could be a florist and I'd still be in love with her.

In love.

God, it feels good to have that thought in my head. It's always there, too. It's an inescapable fact of my life now, and I love that I can't escape it.

CHAPTER NINE

Iris

"Tina," I say as I step into my office. "I take it back. I'm willing to revisit my college experimentation days because I just totally fell in love with you."

She laughs and says, "You've always been in love with me."

I look around and say, "But it's amazing how you got everything up and running so perfectly."

"Not yet," she says. "The copy center will be set up today and you'll be glad to know it will be part of the open floor plan. No closed doors."

I smile and say, "Well, nobody wants me dead anymore but at least I won't have any moments of... uh, phantom fear."

"Phantom? Oh, like phantom pain when someone loses a limb?" I nod and she says, "Iris, stick to being a brilliant businesswoman and leave the remarkable command of the English language to me, okay?"

"You're lucky I love you right now," I say, "or I might have to hold you accountable for this kind of smartassery."

"Assery isn't a word. Once again, I want to encourage you to leave issues of language to me."

I smile and say, "All right, then. Seriously, Tina, great job getting the office up and running. The stuff you found is..." I close the door, "...helpful. The problem is, it's clear that stuff is cherry-picked. What I mean is, it doesn't even come close so we need to get back to find the discrepancy. Any ideas?"

"There are so many damned boxes at the little warehouse, Iris. It's going to take weeks at least, maybe months," she says, "but all I can think to do is just go through it all box by box."

I groan. "The quarter is over next week. I was hoping to figure it out before then. It'll get the loss categorized correctly and finally give us a base point for when we took over."

"And it will also mean the charge-off will happen this quarter and not the first full quarter of you guys taking over."

I chuckle, "Optics are good, too. But it's not that. I want it behind me so they're more receptive to ideas I have about structural changes to procedures."

"Well, I could hire some temps. I haven't called Brinks yet."

"Brinks? Who's that?"

"The guy you replaced," she replies, looking at the computer. "Oh, it's Banks. Sorry. I could call B A N K S, not B R I N K S and maybe he could help narrow the search."

"What do I have going on today?"

"Not a damned thing until four," she says. "The office isn't even supposed to be up and running until Friday so all of the plans were for you to work from home. Four is your conference call but I guess since the office is up now, that might be something you big important very special people have in the conference room."

"Okay, but I'm free until four. Why don't I head over with you? We'll both see what we can find and if we don't get anywhere after a few hours, I'll call Banks for help."

"Ooooh!" she says, "I love when a boss gets hands-on.

I roll my eyes and grab my purse. "You driving or me?"

"I'll drive. I'll need to run to the bank around noon to drop off the credit line receipts. It should only take about an hour."

"Your car it is," I say.

"Of course, I'll milk it so it takes two or three hours and you're stuck looking for the paperwork all by yourself," Tina says, "but it's only fair after all the exhausting work I put in here at the office."

"Sorry," I say with a laugh. "No can do. I'll need you to bring coffee back for me."

We walk to her car, and she continues with the banter about abandoning me. I feel damned good. I feel damned good about work, of course, but I know what's driving my mood at the moment isn't that at all. What's driving my mood is Jeff. When we're in the car and she starts it up, I say, "We told each other I love you a few weeks ago."

She squeals and then says, "Who woulda thunk it? The bad bitch executive finally has her heart melted!"

I laugh and say, "Bad bitch? I don't know why I put up with you."

"Because you've never had any employee as good as me ever before."

"Oh yeah," I say, "that's why." We spend the drive to the storage unit laughing and talking about my new favorite subject, Firefighter Jeff O'Leary. By the time we get there, I'm flying high. She's right about it being more like a small warehouse. In fact, some of the units have signs that suggest business is done out of them. We get to ours and when she rolls up the door I gasp."

"Told ya," she says.

"God," I say, "Why don't you call Banks now and take care of your banking. And we might end up calling for temps, too."

"Your wish is my command," she says with a laugh, "and I'm really happy for you." She gives me a hug and I watch her walk away. I step into the unit and see about eleven rows of file boxes six or seven boxes high. In the back is a door. I check it out. It's a little office only about the size of a walk-in closet. It'll be a good work area, though. I walk back out and grab a box from the first row. In the office, I look through the box. There's nothing relevant to the audit I'm trying to accomplish but there are some documents I set aside to review on unrelated matters.

I go back out and I see Tina. "Back already?" I ask with a smile.

She's not smiling. She looks terrified. "What's wrong?" I ask. She looks like she's on the brink of tears as she steps aside and behind her I see the man holding a gun. "You... you're the one who embezzled from the company. Oh my God."

"It's a good thing all the evidence is about to go up in flames. Sad that the hotshot new director of operations and her assistant got caught in the fire and sadly didn't make it out."

"You'll never get away with this!" I say.

"Spare me the dramatics," he says as he points the gun at Tina and says, "Not one word."

He gestures with the gun and Tina and I step into the closet office. He makes her tie my hands and then he ties hers and forces us to sit. He closes the door behind us and Tina looks at me, too terrified to speak.

CHAPTER TEN

Jeff

I have to tell Iris about my leopard. I love this girl. I love her more than I can even comprehend. I guess when friends fall in love and talk about it, I always think they're overly dramatic about things. I always kind of roll my eyes and act like they're just being childish. Now, though, I can't help myself from thinking along the same lines they do. It feels like from the moment I wake to the moment I sleep; my thoughts are filled with her. Hell, my dreams are filled with her, too. I think in some ways, fear for her safety masks other emotions so they aren't felt as strongly. Now, with that gone, all of my feelings are profoundly strong and very present in my mind.

I love her.

She needs to know the truth.

I let out a roar, which sends birds flying from a nearby

oak. I rarely roar. It really only serves two purposes. If I need to intimidate a threat, a roar is a good way to do it. If I need to frighten prey, a roar does that as well. Now, though, I roar simply because even as a cat, thoughts of Iris fill me and make me desperate for a chance to really show her the true me. She needs to know Jeff O'Leary, the real Jeff O'Leary.

Okay, that's a bullshit way to put it.

She knows me.

She knows exactly who I am.

I have been me with her. I'm always me when I'm with her. Nonetheless, there is a substantially important aspect of my life that... What was the word she used talking about financial reports?

Material.

That's it. Information that would be material to an investor's decision. It's something an investor needs to know in order to make an informed decision.

Being a shifter is material to a relationship. It's not something that can be withheld. She has a right to know about it and I need to tell her. "I'll do it tonight," I say aloud. Then, because I realize I'm full of shit about that, I add, "Damn it! Tell her tonight!"

My voice startles me and I look around. I've shifted back to human just to say those things!

This secret has my insides twisted into knots. "I'll do it tonight," I say and this time I'm full of determination instead of the other stuff. I turn around, shift back, and make my way to the car. I move slowly because I have a four-day shift coming up and that means sleeping at the station. Even though all of the firefighters there are shifters, we're forbidden to shift at the station and I won't be getting out into the wilderness until afterward.

When I get to my car, I shift back and then pull my clothes from inside and put the pile on the hood. I have my boxers and my jeans on when my phone rings from where it rests on the passenger seat.

It's a little confusing to see the number again. I answer with, "Firefighter O'Leary. How may I help you?"

"Jeff," I hear. The captain's voice sounds off. "We had to let him go."

"What?"

"He's not the guy. His alibi checked out."

"Jesus Christ," I say. Then, I get control of myself and say, "Sorry, sir."

"She could have him charged with stalking but the DA says it's a loser. Ultimately, the guy is just creepy. He never actually took any action. He just... God, I don't know, worshipped her from afar."

"Damn it all," I say. Again, I get control of myself. "Thank you for calling me, Captain."

"Son, if you think for one minute, I didn't recognize the look in your eyes, you're wrong. I know you have feelings for her. There might be even more by now. Am I right?"

I sigh. "Yes, Sir."

He can tell in my voice I don't know if that's a problem because he says, "It makes it easy on us, doesn't it? I mean, we're heroes and when we get a chance with someone we were a hero too, it's even better. Look, that's why I called you because I could tell there's something there. So, you could watch out for this guy."

"Any leads on the arson itself?"

He says, "Well, we're going back to the beginning."

"She thinks someone might have been embezzling money before she took over. She thought before you found Derek's letters that maybe the fire was to burn records."

"I'll look into that but that kind of thing usually happens when the offices are empty. A lot of accelerants. You don't want to leave it to chance because you know anything that survives the fire is going to be examined."

"Makes sense," I say. "Well, damn it all. I'll let her know about things and I'll make sure she gets in touch as she researches this embezzlement thing."

"Okay," he says, "and one more thing O'Leary."

"Yes, sir?"

"The offer is still open. The moment you're eligible, if you want to transfer, you're in."

"Thank you, Captain." I hang up and finish getting dressed. I try Iris's phone but it goes to voicemail.

I try her assistance and I hear a whispered, "It's your boyfriend! Hurry, I've got zero battery."

Iris hisses, "Get the police, Jeff. We're at the storage place. Hudson's Ware—"

I stare at the phone. I dial again. Straight to voicemail. I look up Hudson's and there are too many results. I look up Hudson's Storage and fine Hudson's Warehouse and Storage. I'm five minutes away. I hit the gas and dial the police but I hang up before it connects. If Derek is after her, I don't want the police involved at all.

I realize as I pull into the huge complex that I don't know her unit number. I almost call her office with some sort of ruse but I see a car I've seen before. I think it's her assistant's car. I drive next to it and see the open storage unit. A man is there with a can of gasoline, pouring it on the boxes. There's an empty can next to him.

I leap out of the truck and shout, "Fire department! Freeze."

He turns around and that's when I see the gun.

It's a miracle I don't shift. I stop myself as I say, "Tell me what you've done to Tina and Iris."

He smiles and says, "Well now, I can bring you right to them."

He gestures me forward with the gun and has no idea he only has life right now because I need to make sure Iris is okay.

CHAPTER ELEVEN

Iris

I'm surprised to see Jeff when the door opens. Banks tries to push him down but he just steps forward and slides down to a seated position between Tina and me. Banks close the door and I ask, "When will the police be here?"

"I didn't call them," he says. "I'll handle this."

"You'll handle it?" Tina asks.

"You're... what are you saying?" I look at Jeff and try my best not to believe he's just gone insane. "There's no way out."

He shakes his head and says, "I knew I would have to tell you at some point. I wanted to prepare you for it. No time for that now."

"Tell me what?"

"I'm..." He takes a deep breath. "I'm a shifter."

"Holy shit," Tina says, "Really? Oh, that's fucking cool."

"Really," Jeff says.

I'm sure there is something he might have said that might be more shocking to me but at the moment, nothing at all comes to mind. "Oh..." I say in a whisper. *Oh?* What the hell kind of response is that? I don't know a lot about shifters at all. I know they exist, came out into the open about ten years ago. There are still plenty of people who believe their revealing themselves to the world is just a hoax. I don't intend to say what I say next but it comes out, "You should have told me."

It's crazy that it never occurs to me to think he's not telling the truth.

"I know," he said, "and I planned to but—" He stops when I shake my head vehemently.

"You didn't let me finish," I say, "you should have told me but I still love you and nothing is going to change that." He lets out a breath and it seems like I can actually see his stress disappear. "I swear to God, though, Jeff," I say, "I'm totally going to hold this over your head and punish the hell out of you for it."

He chuckles and says, "What if I make it up to you?"

"What do you have in mind?"

"Well, I guess I could save your life right now."

I lean forward and kiss his cheek. "Well, I guess if you do it in a sexy, kind of the badass way it'll help. I mean, it won't get you off the hook completely but I imagine you won't have to spend quite so much on flowers and..."

"Okay, deal," he says.

"Stop interrupting. Flowers and candy and jewelry and movies and dinners out and—"

"Okay," he says. "I get the point. I'll spend the rest of my life spoiling you."

That makes the conversation serious again for me. "Let's make sure there's a rest of your life, Honey," I say.

"My God, you two are so sickeningly sweet I think I'm going to go into diabetic shock," Tina says. "Can you go all beast mode and save us now, please?"

He nods and says, "Back up a little. Both of you."

I slide back and watch him scoot to right in front of the door. Jeff says, "Ordinarily, I'd get undressed first."

Tina says, "I'm up for it." I glare at her and she says, "Joking!"

Jeff says, "Look, this is going to sound crazy to you but be ready. When I shift, my clothes will shred and fly everywhere. The belt buckle could hurt if it flies at you. I want you..."

He can't finish because we hear footsteps outside of the door. "This time you won't be getting away," Banks says as he opens it. He's holding a gas can. "Sorry you got wrapped up in all this," he says to Jeff. "I really like firefighters. I do."

Jeff says, "If you put the can down, you'll walk out of this storage unit. If you don't, you'll be carried out."

Banks laughs. "Well, at least you get to die well and not like a pussy. You know, I think I..."

He doesn't finish.

Jeff's buckle misses me but I do get hit but a button and it feels like a bullet although it doesn't actually enter my body. There's a blur of golden brown and then a giant cat, a leopard I think, has Banks's head in its mouth. I hear the crunching of bone and I don't know if it's the man's skull or his neck breaking. The cat is enormous, and the force of its leap carries both it and Banks out of the closet office. I hear Tina breathe out, "Holly shit," as I scoot to the door and watch.

I only see the thing from behind, although I see Banks's body bouncing around like a ragdoll as the giant animal moves. I lose sight of them around some boxes and I stare nervously at Tina. She says, "God, your boyfriend's badass."

I stare at her and then back where the giant cat was. I look back at Tina and say the first thing that comes to mind. It makes me feel foolish but it's what comes out. "Yeah, totally."

A minute or two later, Jeff is back. He wears jeans. That's it. Tina says, "Yeah, just my luck you've got a pair of pants in your car."

Jeff steps in and a moment later my wrists are untied. Then, Tina's are. Tina throws her arms around him before I can and starts weeping and soon I have my arms around him as well. Both of us weep but he gently pries us off and says, "Listen. There are some things I have to do. I want you guys to leave and pretend this didn't happen. Can you do that for me?"

Tina nods and I say, "When will I see you?"

"I'll come by in a few hours."

"Promise me."

He looks at me and says, "I promise."

He ushers us out to our car. I see Banks's body behind some boxes. I hurry Tina along so she doesn't. Soon, the two of us are at my pace working on our second bottle of wine. Tina finally says, "I don't understand how the coolest day I've ever had can simultaneously be the most screwed up godawful day I've ever had."

I don't know how to respond so I pour more wine.

About an hour and another bottle of wine later, she's sleeping in my guest room and I'm trying to wrap my head around the lethal nature of the man I love. I have no idea how to handle it. I have no idea what we'll do moving forward.

Until the door opens and Jeff steps in. I rush to him and throw my arms around him. He holds me tightly and I whisper, "Is... Did you do what you had to do?"

"It's all over," he says.

"Don't ever tell me what you did," I say.

He kisses my forehead and says, "Okay." Then, he looks at me and says, "Did you mean it?"

I nod. "I don't want to know."

"Not about that. Do you still love me now that you understand what I am?"

I nod, tears in my eyes, and then, as they roll down my cheeks, I say, "Hey, I liked you better without a shirt."

He smiles and kisses me and tells me he can fix that in very short order.

EPILOGUE

Iris

"Is it safe?" I ask. Then, I immediately blurt out, "Oh my God, I'm being totally offensive, aren't I? God, I'm sorry!"

He smiles and reaches forward to stroke my cheek. "It's completely safe. And you're not offensive at all. For God's sake, you saw me tear a man's throat from his neck."

I wince at the memory and say, "Way to reassure me, asshole."

He smiles and says, "Looks like more flowers and jewelry are on the agenda now."

"Don't forget the dinners out and movies."

"Fair enough," he says. He wears only his jeans at the moment and he slides them down to his ankles. He kicks off his shoes and then slides his socks off. He wears boxers now and when he slides them down and stands naked in front of me, I reach out and take hold of his cock. He lets out a moan and then says, "Jesus. Why the hell would you do that now?"

"Just giving you the motivation to shift back afterward," I giggle.

"Motivation accomplished," he says.

I give him a stroke and pull my hand away. "You're lucky you turn fully human when you shift back because there's no way I'd let you stick a cat dick in me. I went online and found out they're full of thorns."

"Well, barbs, but..." I raise an eyebrow and he says, "...and I'm going to stop talking now."

"Smart boy," I say. All of the nervousness comes back and I say, "let me back up."

He nods and I take two steps backward. Then, I take a third. I stop and after about fifteen or twenty seconds, he says, "Are you ready?" I nod and he says, "Okay."

And then he's gone.

There's an enormous leopard instead.

It all happens so fast it almost looks like Jeff disappears and the giant cat appears. At the same time, though, I see his body change. It just happens so quickly, like a movie sped up to an impossible degree. I stare at the beast in front of me. My first thought is that it's big.

Jesus, it's huge!

It's bigger than anything I've ever seen at a zoo. For God's sake, it looks bigger than a horse or even a rhino. I don't have any idea how to wrap my head around its size, and everything feels a bit surreal when the enormous leopard turns its giant head to look at me. I gasp and feel my heart beat faster than it even seems capable of beating.

And then, I see the leopard's eyes.

They don't look like Jeff's eyes, at least not physically, but they still look like Jeff. "Oh," I say in a whispered voice of wonder. "Oh, Honey! It is you." I feel the weight of the big cat's head on my shoulder before I realize I stepped forward and put my arms around him. I stroke his neck and his shoulders and it's almost overpowering, the very obvious strength in this creature, strength that ought to terrify me, along with the certainty that I'm safe with it.

Safe with Jeff.

Not a creature.

Not an it.

Jeff.

The one I love.

Suddenly, he's a man again and I smile at him and say, "Yes."

"Yes?"

"I'll marry you."

He lifts his hands and says, "You accepted my proposal last week."

I reach out and stroke his cheek, fixating a bit on the ring on my finger. "Yeah, but now, I mean it," I say.

He smiles and says, "You know, Tina's wrong about me. In this relationship, you're the badass one."

"Well don't forget it, spot-boy."

"Spot boy? Are you serious?"

"Don't get catty with me."

"Oh my God," he says, "Is this my new reality?"

"Stop being such a pussy."

"Dear Lord, seriously?"

I giggle and kiss his cheek. "You know, I think I might like it better if you had whiskers. What do you say I make you purr?"

"Leopards don't purr. We don't have..."

His words disappear as my fingers wrap around his cock. "Really?" I ask. "I beg to differ."

DID you like *Lusty Leopard's Fiery Girl*? I really enjoyed writing this one, and I think Iris is definitely on her way to a real happily ever after life with Firefighter O'Leary. I loved writing her character. For me, the idea of a woman who is not only romantic and loving but also incredibly strong and professional is really appealing. I have to admit I fell in love with Jeff. Of course, I'm a sucker for shifters and a total sucker for firemen.

You're going to love the next visit to Company 417!

There's nobody better when the blaze is uncontrollable than Fort Gilmore. He's fearless and a natural leader in a crisis. If there's a fire and everything is chaotic, he knows what to do. This wolf shifter makes a decision and makes it happen. Then, he runs into Carmella Grant, and he decides exactly what he wants. He wants her. The problem is, someone else wants Carmella, too, and that very dangerous man isn't interested in how she feels about it. Can Fort save Carmella from a psychopath who's already claimed her? Even if he can, what will she do when she finds out he's just as much a wolf as man? Find out in *Reckless Wolf's Dangerous Liaison*, the new exciting paranormal romance in the *Company 417 Shifters* series!

In Love with the Enemy

Love for you Alone

A Rizer Wolfpack Series BOX SET

Rune Series

Rune Sword

Rune Master

Rune Hunter

Rune King's Daughter

Rune Romance Complete Series BOX SET

SENSUAL ABDUCTION SERIES

Aeon Captive

Aeon Fugitive

Aeon War

Aeon Ending

Sensual Abduction Series Box Set

Unbearable Romance Series: Bearly Deniable

Hunting for Love

The Soul of a Bear

UnBearable Romance Series

THE ADNA PLANET SERIES

Baston

Sca

Ruby

The Adna Planet Series Box Set

The Blue Falls Series: Rival Love

Strong Love

Magic Love

The Blue Falls Series

THE AVROXEE MATES SERIES

Prisoner of Avrox

Champion of Avrox

Secrets of Avrox

The Avroxee Mates Series BOX SET

The Galaxy Smugglers Series: Forbidden Delivery

Forbidden Reunion

Forbidden Territory